Something
To
Someone

ISBN 0-935906-03-7

This book is written

For those wishing
  To know someone special
While seeking the greater challenge
  To know themselves

we are given life

We are all born into this World with certain abilities and various needs. The challenge of Life is for us to discover those abilities and to use them, while fulfilling our needs. Each person must do this within the realm of a completely unique set of circumstances. Our abilities are as many and varied as there are people, but we will find that our needs are common to all. The need that offers the greatest potential for joy is also the need that offers the greatest potential for pain, the need to share our life with someone.

I don't wish to be
  Everything to Everyone
But I would like to be
Something to Someone

Again last night you came to me
With tales of the end of your latest romance
Asking how could you possibly bear the pain
With your head on my shoulder
I dried your tears
While assuring you that tomorrow
Someone new would come along
When you were finally comforted
You kissed my cheek
And returned to your world

As I looked around the apartment
Now empty again
I thought of my walks in the park
Watching the couples
Of tables for one
And movies alone
And as I reached for the T.V. Guide
I felt the moisture of a tear
Running down my face

For while some people have
A shoulder to cry on
It is the destiny of others
That they must cry alone

So many are afraid
   of the word "Hello"
Because so often it leads
   to the word "Goodbye"

So often I hear it from others
Others who are struggling
To make their relationship
What it should be naturally

Yet they don't hesitate to say
"With so many people out there
Surely you can find someone"

But my problem lies in the fact
That I don't want just someone
I want the right Someone

And a chance to grow

Sometimes the World
Is willing to give
At a time that we are not
Ready to receive

So often we reach out
And offer that which we have to give
To someone who has no need
Or does not recognize the value of our gift
Thus our gift goes unreceived
Through no fault of our own
And this rejection causes pain

But the real tragedy occurs
When someone comes along
Who has a need for
And recognizes the value
Of what we have to give
But because the memory of rejection
Is still fresh on our mind
We are no longer
Reaching out

Not everyone knows how to give
But then—
  Not everyone knows how to receive

It's so easy
  To think about Love
  To talk about Love
  To wish for Love
But it's not always easy
  To recognize Love
    Even when we hold it
    In our hands

We should not expect
More from others
Than we are willing
To give to ourselves

The only acceptance we truly need
Is Self-Acceptance
For once we have gained that
The rest should come
And that which does not come
Will not matter

I am a collection of characteristics
Both physical and mental
That makes me completely unique
No one else anywhere
Is exactly like me
And I realize that not everyone
Who crosses my path
Will be interested
In what I have to offer

But my strength comes
From the belief
That Someone
Somewhere

Can and Will
Appreciate me
For what I am

Some people
   Think too highly of others
   And not enough of themselves

While many
   Think too highly of themselves
   And not enough of others

We should always remember
—To themselves
  No one is just another person

Our lives will know sunshine

Touch gently the Life
Of your fellow man
For the human heart
Shapes as easily
As clay upon
The potter's wheel

Please give me the ability

To understand
To be more than just—another man
To accomplish all the things
I was sent here to do
And to touch the World gently
As I pass through

Being Human
I will make mistakes
I will say things that shouldn't be said
I will do things that shouldn't be done
And these things will bring pain
To myself and unfortunately others

But when the time comes
That I have hurt enough
To ask forgiveness from God above
And understanding from my fellow man
Then I will have the strength
To continue
Being Human

So often Life
Is not filled
With Love and Laughter
As much as
With Loneliness and Disappointment

But there will be enough
Of those beautiful moments
With very special people
To make it all
Seem worthwhile

It's not easy
This thing called Life
With its broken dreams
And lonely nights
And all the things
That don't work out right

It would be easier
If it came with a script
Of who we were to meet
And the right things to say
And nothing but sunshine
Filling each day

Yes, it would be easier
But it wouldn't be Life

I reach out to the World
A World that has given me Life
A World that has given me Dreams
And I pray
That I might have the Courage
To explore my Life
To Live my Dreams

No one can determine who I am
But myself
My parents can not
My teachers can not
My friends can not

They can guide me
But in the final analysis
The problem is completely mine
For I have abilities
That are completely unique to me
And the challenge of Life
Is for me
To discover them
To develop them
To use them

For then and only then
Will I know
Who I Am

What a price we pay for experience
When we must sell our youth to buy it

One day I said to God—

I'm going to search
For the meaning to my existence
I'm going to find the talent within me
Then develop it to the best of my ability
And I'm going to make the most of this Life
That I have been given

And I'm going to do this
Without infringing upon anyone else's
Opportunity to do the same

And God replied
"I couldn't ask for anything more"

I'm not very good
At this Game called Life
For I've not learned to see children crying
Without feeling pain
For I've not learned to watch animals destroyed
Without wondering why
For I've not yet met a king or celebrity
That I would bow down to
Or a man so insignificant
That I would use for a stepping-stone
For I've not learned to be a "yes man"
To narrow minded bosses
Who quote rules without reason
And I've not learned to manipulate
The feelings of others
To be used for my own advantages
Then cast aside as I see fit

No, I'm not very good
At this Game called Life
And if everything goes well
Maybe I never will be

At the end of each day
We should be
One step closer
To what we should be

But also some rain

I've noticed a paradox
In this cold world where strangers seldom speak
And Heaven forbid should they ever touch
But on a dance floor when slow music plays
Two strangers can come together
Without questions
Without lies
And while the music is playing
They can express a basic human need
To hold
And be held

And somehow I can't help but believe
That the whole world
Should learn to play
A little more
''Slow Music''

When the music slowed
  I crossed the crowded room
    And reached out to her
She came without hesitation
  Not as a stranger
    Who had shared only a smile
She placed her hand in mine
  Her head on my shoulder
    And her body close to mine
As the music played
  I could feel her trembling
    From all the loneliness inside
Yet we never spoke
  For there really wasn't anything
    That needed to be said
When the song ended
  She returned to her world
    And I to mine
Now after all the years
  I will occasionally close my eyes
    And relive those few moments
      That we shared

You can know someone better
In a moment of Honesty
Than ever you can
In a lifetime of Lies

Strangers are people
  Whose paths have never crossed
  And no common time
    Has ever been shared
But once this happens
  They can never truly
  Be strangers again

Have you ever noticed
    That strangers become uneasy
    When silence comes between them
    For they immediately start worrying
    What the other is thinking

For we usually need
    To know someone very well
    Before we can feel comfortable
    With their silence

As the moon floated across the sky
And twinkled in the ripples in the lake
I sat silently beside you
And tossed pebbles into the water
From time to time you would squeeze my hand
And rest your head on my shoulder
There was no radio
No television
No pennies for your thoughts

Funny how quickly the hours passed
And how much closer I felt to you
Maybe more often
We should sit down together
And have a good, long ``Silence''

I've been touched by the morning sun
  That chases the night away
And I've been touched by the gentle words
  That love-struck poets say
And I've been touched by the morning mist
  Everyone calls the dew
But it all seems more beautiful
  Now that I've been touched by you

I've noticed
That being with you
I smile a little more often
I anger a little less quickly
The sun shines a little brighter
And life is so much sweeter

For being with you
Takes me to a different place
A place called Love

Our path is a little clearer
Our steps are a little lighter
And we appear a little taller
When we walk beside
Someone we Love

If you should need
Someone to talk to
A shoulder to lean on
I'll be there

And if you should need
Time to yourself
Your own space
I'll step back
To give you room

But you must realize
That I need your help
If I am to know
Exactly what you need

Some couples have learned
   To communicate with words
Some have learned
   To communicate with actions
While others have even learned
   To communicate with silence

Yet there are so many
   Who have never learned
      To communicate at all

Hard times will make us strong

If there must be pain
Then let it be my pain
For it would be easier to bear
Any pain that you might give
Than the pain I would feel
In knowing that
I had hurt you

There is no one
Who can hurt me
Like myself
For I can take a simple statement
And twist it around in my mind
Till my body trembles with pain
And I wonder how anyone
Could be so cruel
To say such a thing

Yes, given enough time
My imagination
Can make the proverbial mountain
Out of a molehill

Even if I'm hurting today
I'll look foward to tomorrow
For there's a very thin line
Between happiness and sorrow

Many people wish
  They could change their life
When all they need to do
  Is change their attitude
  Toward Life

The quality of a person's life
Does not depend on the circumstances
Of his life
As much as the attitude
With which he faces those circumstances

It seems that Life
Could be compared to a giant jigsaw puzzle
With each person like each piece
Having a place where they fit perfectly
Yet so many in there need to belong
Grab the first place they come to
Then try to make it fit

And because of this
They are never quite in harmony
With their adjoining pieces
Thus they never get to know
The way it was truly
Meant to be

In areas of Life
  Where reason controls
  We usually learn
    From our mistakes.

Unfortunately
  This is not always true
    In areas where emotion controls

I can live with
  Because I can learn from
  The pain I feel
    When something I do wrong
    Causes someone special
    To leave my life

But the pain that's doubly
  Hard to bear
    Comes when I lose someone
    Without even
    Knowing why

To Someone
We represent the possibility
Of an end to lonely nights
Of dreams come true
A chance for Happiness

But we also represent
The possibility of long nights
Of wondering—
What went wrong

And someday someone new might come along

I thought it funny when they asked
If I felt cheated now that I've lost you
For I could have lost you
Only if I had owned you
The way I might own a coin

But you are another person
Traveling through life
And I was lucky just to have shared
A part of your journey

So how could I feel cheated
When there are so many
Who have never known you
At all

From time to time
Two paths will cross
Then merge together
To appear to be one
And as such will travel
Many miles

But so often
The fortunes of the world
Make it necessary
For them to separate
In order to reach
Their own destinations

I didn't ask for it to be over
  But then again
    I didn't ask for it to begin
For that's the way it is with Life
As some of the most beautiful days
  Come completely by chance
But even the most beautiful days
  Eventually have their sunset

The pain we feel
  When someone leaves our life
Is in direct proportion
  To the joy they bring
  While a part of our life

For a few moments
 In my Life
You made me feel
 As if I truly meant
  Something to Someone

I won't say I miss you
But my pillow answers to your name now

And offer us the chance to be

Something to Someone

I would like to thank the thousands of people who have taken the time to write. The letters have meant much to me; however, due to the volume and the way I have been traveling the past several years, it has not been possible to answer every letter. My apologies for this.

If you need extra copies of "Something To Someone" or the first two books, "Footprints In the Mind" and "Meet Me Halfway," please check with your favorite local bookstore. If they do not have them in stock, they probably can get copies from their supplier. You might also ask them to contact me directly at the address below, or you can contact me directly for the current price list and ordering information.

Thanks and Best Wishes
Javan
P.O. Box 1828
Cumming, Georgia 30130

Javan was born October 19, 1946 in Thomasville, N.C. He lived in Charlotte, N.C. through his school years, then moved to Atlanta in 1968 where he worked as a gate agent for Eastern Airlines until 1977. In 1979 he published his first book and started the difficult process of getting the stores around the nation to stock it. Now after five years of traveling, he is working on his dream home on forty acres at a lake north of Atlanta.

Soon he hopes to be able to travel internationally, and to continue his hobbies of photography and various types of aviation.

Javan is the author's given middle name. He pronounces it Je vahn.

I wink you're thunderful

But I can't thay it wery vell

If there is someone you think is wonderful and you can't say it very well, then this book just might be especially for you.